THE STRANGERS

NITHILA

Contents

PREFACE

Thank you again for picking up this book.

I have always been a fan of myster, crime, thriller and horror. I started my writing as a hobby, writing articles related to mental health, psychology and true crime. And when the idea to write a short story popped up, i wanted to give it a try. This story was sitting in my folders for months and I decided to publish it and give it a shot. This is my first time writing a story and I hope it reaches to your expectations.

Have a happy reading!

I

Birds chirped on that Wednesday morning as a young woman climbed up the white marble stairs and opened the milky cream white door and the smell of raspberry reed diffuser hit her nose. She moved to the cherry red bed where a figure was tangled in the white sheets with a panda plushie in her grip and her hair sprawled over the pillows. She bent down to wake up her little sister.

"Willow, wake up. It's time for school" my sister whispered in my ears. I pulled the covers over my head and turned to the other side and mumbled a "no" to my sister. "Baby, wake up, please! If you wake up, I will get you an ice cream" she cooed in my ears, but I refused to budge. She climbed on the bed and slid under the covers and started tickling me.

I started giggling as she tickled me and immediately shot up from the bed and shouted, "Okay! I'm up" I said while laughing and trying to catch my breath. "Ah! Finally!" my sister told with a playful grin on her face. "Okay, now get up and get ready for school," she said while kissing my forehead and getting up from the bed to go downstairs.

Once she closed the doors I got up, put the covers and pillow in their place, and walked towards the bathroom to refresh myself.

After a bath, I wore a yellow hoodie that read Hope and a pair of black jean to match it. I put my hair into a ponytail and put the required books into my bag and skipped downstairs where my brother was preparing breakfast. I tiptoed towards him and back-hugged him saying "Good Morning".

"Good morning potato," he said while ruffling my hair.

"Hey! I just now combed my hair" I whined at him and said, "And don't call me a potato" as I glared at him.

"Aww! But I love calling you that baby sis" he told as he took the prepared dishes to the table to eat. I went and punched him in the shoulders and said "I hate you". He looked at me and pulled me into a hug as he said "But I know you love me". I smiled in his embrace because that is always the truth.

My sister came to the table as she finished talking on the phone and sat on the chair and began serving the food for us. My brother and I sat on the chair and started eating the delicious food prepared by my brother. Once we finished eating, my brother cleaned the dishes and I filled my water bottle to leave for school. My sister came dressed in a peach-colored shirt and a black pencil skirt, ready to leave for her work. My brother, after cleaning the utensils, went up to get ready for work. Once he came down, I waved them goodbye and kissed their cheeks, and left for school while they left for their companies in their respective cars.

I was walking to my school, which was 15 min away from my home. Even though my brother volunteered to leave me at school before his work I refused because I loved walking as I enjoy the fresh air and I am a nature lover. I love watching people from different walks of life strolling in the streets of Birmingham, some rushing to catch a bus for work, and people bustling into the trendy cafes for their morning dose of coffee and sugar. We have been living in Birmingham since my brother's birth. Birmingham is my home.

My brother and sister mean the world to me. My brother, Mark, has his own company, Personascape, where he provides interior designs for companies, hotels, and houses. My sister, Amelia, owns a clothing brand, Serendipity, which is very popular with celebrities. She works with many models and has designed a lot of dresses for fashion shows.

My parents are millionaires, most of the time, they're away for work. My dad, Alex Turner, owns RoboCorps, where they provide robots to common people, especially the elderly, where the robots help them with household chores and also act as a companion to them. The company also provides robots to other companies and police departments. He has branches all over the world hence he is required to travel a lot. My mom, Gracie Turner, has a publishing company called Vintage, where she has published a lot of magazines and books. She too has many branches around the world.

My mom always follows my dad wherever he goes, hence I don't see them often. I miss them a lot. But whenever they come, we always have family outings and picnics, making happy memories.

I reached my school gates and entered along with the crowd. Being in the final year of school was very stressful with lots of assignments and exams on the way and also preparing for university admission. Once I entered the hallway, I saw my best friend, Lisa, waiting for me. Once she saw me her face brightened up and a wide smile appeared on her face. "Hey, friend! Ready for the exam?" she called out to me and put her hand around my shoulders. I smiled at her and said "Hey! Yeah, let's do this" as we walked to our classes with the bell ringing in the background signaling us to enter into our respective rooms.

...

II

A young man is sitting on a worn-out couch with an Apple laptop that was recently stolen from a gadget store. His screen displays statistics and stock values belonging to four companies. With a cigarette in his mouth, he is monitoring the values and details of the companies. He sees a shadow moving beside him and looks up from the screen to see his sister standing with her hands on her hips. She was of medium height, with black hair with caramel highlights and attractive blue eyes. She pulled the cigarette from his mouth and put it down and stomped it as she glared at him. "I told you to not smoke inside the home. Can you at least listen to me once?" she asked with annoyance laced in her voice. He rubbed his face as if trying to rub the exhaustion and dark circles that settled on his face from long hours of staring at the laptop and sleepless nights. "Okay" he replied and moved his gaze back to the screen and she rolled her eyes and walked away to the kitchen.

She brought four bowls of soup from the kitchen and kept them on the table and went inside the room to call their parents for dinner. They were a family of four living in a one-bedroom apartment. The siblings gave the room to the parents and they slept in the living room where two couches were put beside each other. With tight finances, the family was living on a meal-to-meal basis. The brother worked in a mechanic shop and the sister worked in a convenience store in the evening hours and as a babysitter in the morning hours. Even with multiple jobs, they were unable to pay the bills on time and debts were also increasing gradually.

She went to her brother and called him for dinner. He kept the laptop on the couch and got up and walked to the dining table. All of them were eating the dinner silently, with only the slurping noise of the soup being heard.

The father broke the silence and asked the son" Have you prepared the plan?". The son looked up from the bowl at his father and replied" Yes, I am looking at the company details and creating a summary. Once I have prepared it for the four companies, I will brief you guys on it and we can move to the next step in our plan".

The father nodded and took one more spoon of his soup, while thinking about something and said" Our plan should be perfect, I won't accept any mistakes. This is our only way to live the dream life we have always wanted to create".

The son nodded "I know dad, don't worry. I have everything planned perfectly. I am just looking for the perfect opportunity to put the plan into action" he said as he gazed into the emptiness, with eyes swirling with darkness and mind already concocting his next plan.

...

III

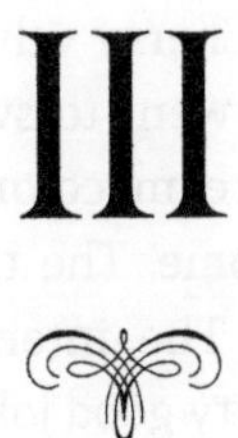

The bell rang indicating that my last period had ended and I can finally head home. Once the teacher went out of the class, Lisa and I packed our bags and went out into the hallways, which were filled with chatters and laughter.

As we were walking to the entrance Lisa looked at me with hopeful eyes and asked" Willow, can we go to the newly opened ice cream shop?". I looked at the time and it was 4 PM leaving me with enough time to go to the ice cream shop. My siblings will usually be back by 6 PM before which I should be at home. I turned to Lisa and said" Yeah sure! I wanted to go there for a long time" with excitement laced in my voice and we walked towards the new shop.

We went to the ice cream shop, Cherry on Top, and it was a small and cute shop with a pink aesthetic theme. There were many students from our school, most of them being couples. We ordered two ice creams, Neapolitan with cherry-bursting boba as toppings and Mint chocolate chip with Oreo pieces as toppings. We ate the ice creams slowly savoring the taste and talking about recent TV shows that we were binge-watching.

At 5:30 PM I reached my home leaving Lisa a street before where there was a bus stand for her to reach home.

She lived 30 minutes away from the school.

I unlocked the door entered the dark home and locked the door. I came to the Cherry velvet couch and threw my bag and keys on it and went to switch on the lights. The lights were of milky cream color hence giving a white aesthetic look to our home. The theme of our home was cherry red and white. The interior design was by my brother and he did a pretty good job.

I went to my room and refreshed myself and went down to get myself something to eat. I like to eat healthy snacks so I picked the Greek yogurt and mixed some grapes with it and came and sat on the couch. I switched on the TV and started sifting through the channels. My phone just then lit up and rang with my mother's name popping up on the screen. I immediately muted the TV and picked up the call and answered.

"Hello, mom! How are you? I miss you so much" I talked with happiness laced in my voice without letting her talk.

She chuckled and replied," I miss you too baby! Don't worry your dad and I are coming to Birmingham next week and we will be staying there for about a month".

I was excited and squealed into the phone at the happy news. I was so eager to meet them.

" This is awesome! I am so happy mom. I can't wait to meet you guys" I told her with an excited and happy voice.

My mom then asked about my day and how school was going and generally how I was.

With all the excitement and happiness, I failed to notice the figure standing at the kitchen window staring at me.

...

I was working in my room on my final assignment on personality disorders. I heard the front door being unlocked indicating that my siblings are back home. I went downstairs to greet my siblings. I ran to them and hugged them both.

"Hey, I have good news. Mom and Dad are coming home!" I said with an excited voice and wearing a wide smile on my face.

Even though their eyes look tired, I could see their eyes brighten upon hearing the news.

"Wow! Finally, they're coming back after six months!" my brother said with relief and excitement settling on his face.

"I know right, I miss them a lot," my sister said as she stared at the family photo hanging on the wall.

My sister and brother went to their respective rooms to freshen up and came downstairs for dinner. I wanted to prepare grilled vegetables, so I started cutting vegetables and my brother joined me in the kitchen to make some pasta for us. After we ate dinner, my brother was watching the news while my sister and I were curled up on the couch beside our brother and scrolling through our phones. My siblings were tired from all the intense work in their companies so they went to their room early to take a rest.

I washed the utensils and cleaned up the kitchen before going back to my room. As I went to switch off the lights of the kitchen, I saw through the kitchen window that the security at the front gate was missing. I was confused because the security guard never misses a day for work. And even if he was going to take time off from work, he would inform us before his leave.

"Probably he had informed my siblings" I mumbled to myself as I turned and walked towards my room. I came into the room and closed the door, as cool air flowed into the room giving me goosebumps on my arms and ruffling my hair. I saw that one of the windows was left open. I was confused and scared at the same time because I never leave my windows open unless I feel the need to breathe some fresh air while studying. Most of the time my air conditioner would be on, so I won't be opening the windows. I immediately went and latched the window and looked around my room if anything is unusual. Once I checked if everything is alright, I climbed onto my bed and slid under the covers, and not thinking too much about the issue, I slipped into dreamland failing to notice the figure under my bed through the mirror.

...

It was already the weekend and the young man was sitting on the couch sipping on his coffee and scrolling through the phone. His father came out of the room while putting on his glasses and sat on the couch beside his son. He took the remote and switched on the TV. He was changing the channels until the news channel came and settled on watching it. He turned to his son who had his eyes trained on his phone.

"Are you ready with the next step?" he asked his son as he kept his eyes on the news flashing on the TV screen.

"I have a plan. I just need the perfect opportunity to put it into action. Let's keep preparing for the D-day and everything will be alright. I will find some- "his speech was cut when they heard the news anchor talk about two people and this brought an evil smirk on his face. He looked at his father's face who also had an evil grin on his face.

"Now we have the perfect plan," the young man said as both son and father laughed deviously at their plan.

•

I twisted in my bed as I woke up from the sunlight falling on my face making me squint my eyes from the sudden brightness. Just then I heard the door of my room open and saw my sister coming towards me to wake me up.

When she saw me trying to open my eyes completely, she chuckled and said "Good morning! Your brother and I already had our breakfasts since we have meetings to attend. We have kept the breakfast on the table, so eat properly and go to meet Lisa. Okay?"

I nodded and mumbled an okay while getting up from the bed. My sister kissed my forehead and left the room. I freshened up and wore and a black hoodie with Savage written on it and blue ripped jeans to match it. I went down and gulped my breakfast quickly since I had only 20 minutes left to go and meet Lisa. I went out and locked the door and walked towards the gate and found the security guard still missing. Hmm, that's weird I thought to myself and walked to the cute café that opened last month, Latte Love.

As I was walking, I heard footsteps behind me and I assumed it must be someone walking in the same direction. Once I came to an intersection where I had to cross, I looked beside me to see who was walking beside me and I found no one. This ignited a small fear inside me. But I heard footsteps behind me, then how did the person disappear? I brushed it off as I crossed the street and started walking on the pavement that was decorated with pink blossom trees.

As I was walking while looking at the trees, I heard footsteps behind me. Suppressing the urge to turn back and look at the person I started walking faster. My heart rate was shooting up and I was nervous and scared. There was a small alleyway which I had to cross to reach the café. I increased my pace and just when I reached the end of the alleyway, I felt a hand on my shoulder. I panicked and pushed away from the hand and screamed, only to turn around and see an empty alleyway. The person who followed me once again disappeared.

Without wasting another minute, I rushed to the café and closed the door, and went in. Lisa was sitting on a comfy couch in the corner while scrolling through her phone. I went and sat opposite her. She immediately looked up and smiled at me but slowly she started frowning at me.

"Willow? Are you okay? You look as if you saw a ghost" she said with a worried tone.

"It's nothing. I just felt like someone was following me but then when I checked no one was there" I said as I nervously fiddled with my fingers while I look out into the beginning of the forests.

"Hey, don't worry. I think you are stressed with all the work we have. Everything will be alright" Lisa told as she looked at me staring out of the windows.

I wish everything will be alright, but I know what I heard wasn't my imagination but the truth. Because right now I was looking at the figure hidden in the darkness of the forest staring right at me.

...

"Willow......Willow......WILLOW!" Lisa shouted at me and I was brought out of my trance.

"Willow are you okay? You have been staring at that forest for so long" she said as her face contorted with worry.

"Yeah, I am fine. Sorry I was just distracted "I told her as she started picking out the required study materials and I looked at the forest again and saw no one.

I decided to push away the matter and start focusing on my studies for the time being. We sat and revised for about three hours, in between we ordered some Strawberry Pudding Cheesecake Cookies and a Vanilla Sweet Cream Cold Brew. By the time we finished studying it was one in the afternoon. We packed everything and left for our home.

When I reached home the door was already unlocked. I entered and saw my brother sitting on the couch and working on his laptop.

"Hey, what are you doing at home?" I asked as I removed my shoes and put the keys on the key hanger.

"Oh hey, you're back? I didn't have any meetings so I thought I will come back home and if needed, work from here" he told as he closed the laptop and went to the kitchen.

"Shall I get you something to eat?" he asked as he peeped into the fridge for the ingredients.

"No, I ate in the café and my stomach is full. I am going up to sleep" I told him and went up the stairs to my bedroom.

After refreshing myself I went and slid into the covers. The thought of the strange man sent shivers down my spine, giving me a bad vibe. The feeling of something wrong about to happen was nagging me and I didn't like it one bit. I forced myself to not think about it and drifted off to sleep.

I spent the remaining day and the next day in my room, completing assignments and studying for the upcoming exams. My brother and sister were cooped up in their rooms working on their laptops and attending calls.

Monday morning soon came and today my parents will be coming home. I'm so excited and happy, that I can't wait for it to be already evening. As usual, my sister came to wake me up and we had breakfast and I left for school while they left for work.

The whole day I was thrumming with excitement and never once remembered the strange man from yesterday. The moment I heard the last bell ring I pulled Lisa with me and ran through the corridors to the gate. Once we reached outside the scene in front of me was shocking.

My mom, dad, brother, and sister were standing on the other side waiting for me. I didn't expect them to come to my school. I was so happy and waved a bye to Lisa and ran across the road to hug my parents. But before I could reach her my mom's face turned into one of horror as she shouted my name, before I could register what was going on I was slammed by an enormous force on my right side and flew a few meters away and fell on the road.

My whole right side and my head were aching with tremendous pain and I watched my blood flow on the concrete road. Just before I closed my eyes, I saw my parents and siblings run toward me with tears running down their faces.

...

Willow was rushed to the hospital and she was taken into the Intensive care unit while the parents and siblings waited outside with fear and worry gripping their hearts. They waited for about 3 hours without moving an inch from their seats. The red light that indicated an ongoing operation was switched off. The doctor came out and called the family to meet him in his room. The family went to the room on the second floor, which was cream yellow with pastel green furniture. The doctor sat down on his seat and asked the parents to take a seat too.

"We have operated on the patient and with regards to her brain injury, she has an internal hemorrhage leading to the swelling of the brain. So right now, she is in a coma, we aren't sure how long she would be in a coma, it might be days, weeks, months, or even years" he said as he gave the reports to the family.

The mother and sister were sobbing silently while the brother and the father were struggling to keep their tears at bay. They thanked the doctor and walked out of the room. For days each member of the family used to sit beside the unconscious Willow and talk to her about their day, asking her to come back, hoping she could listen to them and wake up.

•

I could feel my body burning with pain. I heard the doctors rushing me to the Intensive care unit. As they injected me with anesthesia, I felt myself drowning in the depths of the darkness. I felt the cold air touching my body, and someone's hand holding mine. I recognized the voice to be my mother's, but I couldn't understand what she was talking about. The voice sounded very distant and muffled. For days I could feel the agonizing pain, even though they administered enough pain medications and my family was always there in the room. I wanted to hold their hand, be able to talk to them but I couldn't move an inch. I was floating in the darkness and trapped inside my body without any escape.

•

Six months later

I could feel the warmth of someone's hands on my arm and the sound of the air conditioner. I tried to move my arm and I could feel my little finger twitch slightly. I was so happy as I kept trying to move my hands and open my eyes. Slowly I opened my eyelids and the sudden brightness of the room created a sting in my eye. I immediately closed it and I heard my sister calling my name in a happy voice. I slowly opened my eyes and let them adjust to the surroundings and grasped my sister's hand. Finally, I came out of the darkness, I was so happy and I started tearing up when I turned my head and saw my sister crying happy tears as she saw me. I saw my parents and brother entering the room with smiles on their faces and tears in their eyes.

Immediately after my parents came in, the doctor entered and checked up on me. He told my parents that I can be discharged once I start walking. After the doctors left, I spent some cozy time with my family, and the next week every day I walked for some time in the garden in the hospital. Many patients come there for walking and sit on the bench to get some fresh air.

After a week, I was discharged and I went back home with my brother and sister. Once I entered the home my mom and dad came and hugged me with big smiles on their face. I smiled and kissed their cheeks and went up to my room to take some rest. The medications made me drowsy and half the time I wanted to sleep. Once I laid myself on the bed and snuggled into the sheets, I fell asleep immediately.

The next morning, I woke up to the loud sound of music from the living room. Hmm, that's weird.........we never play music loud, since all of us prefer silence in the house. I got up, freshened up, and went down to see what was going on.

When I went down, I saw my sister wearing a red silk shirt tucked into a pair of blue jean. She was swaying her body to the music and cooking something in the kitchen. I was taken aback by seeing the scene in front of me because my sister never wears jeans to her company since she considers jeans as informal. And she likes listening to music but she doesn't like to dance. I was confused by the sudden change in her behavior......maybe she changed over these six months? I asked myself and moved towards her.

When she turned towards me my jaw dropped. She was wearing red matte lipstick and had applied thick eyeliner to her eyes. My sister only wears light makeup when she goes to a party otherwise, she isn't fond of makeup.

Something was wrong and I didn't have a good feeling about it.

...

"Hey, sis! How are you?" she asked me with an excited voice.

"Hey! I am good......Umm.........You usually don't wear makeup, right?" I asked with surprise and confusion laced in my voice.

She nervously laughed and turned towards the stove to switch it off.

"Umm...I have something to tell you. When you were unconscious, those months were the most difficult to handle. Two months after the accident I met a guy and I fell in love and we started going to parties and dates. He introduced many people to me and the girls and I got very close. So, I started putting on makeup often along with my newfound friends." she replied nervously.

I am happy for her, but I don't want to lie that I am not upset. In my absence so much has happened and I feel like I don't know the person standing in front of me. She must have gone through so much to change like this.

I smiled at her and hugged her." I am so happy for you. I want to meet that guy soon" I told her and winked.

She smiled and replied, "Soon".

She proceeded to go call my brother and parents for breakfast.

My parents and brother came to the dining hall. My brother was busy on his phone while my parents had a wide smile on their faces once they saw me.

"My daughter, how are you?" my mother asked as she sat down to eat.

"I am okay, mom. I missed you guys so much" I said as I teared up.

"Ahh, no crying princess. We only want you to smile" my dad said from across the table.

After we finished eating, we cleaned the leftover food and the table. My brother and sister were getting ready to go to the company and my parents left for their respective companies.

From the moment I woke up my brother hasn't glanced at me even once. Confused and upset by his behavior I walked toward his room and knocked on the door before opening it. He was sitting on the corner of the bed, fully dressed up and texting someone on his phone. I walked up to him from behind and hugged his neck. He immediately pushed me away and got up suddenly with anger on his face.

"Are you blind? Can't you see I am busy? Why do you have to be so clingy?" he asked as he took his laptop and put it in his bag and grabbed his keys.

I was standing there shocked by his outburst and tears pooled in my eyes. As he walked fast to the door, he stopped and took a deep breath. He turned and walked toward me.

"Hey, I am sorry. I shouldn't have shouted at you. I'm extremely stressed due to work. Please forgive me?" he asked as he wiped the tears that ran down my face. I simply nodded at him while he gave me a small smile and walked away.

As a family, we had a promise that we will never show our anger or stress related to work at home. But today, seeing my brother break the rule he came up with, surprises me. I guess these six months have changed my brother and sister a lot and I completely hate it. Thankfully my parents haven't changed.

Just the thought of my brother and sister used to make me warm and happy, but now I feel uneasy and a nagging feeling that makes me anxious.

...

After the unpleasant event with my brother, I went back to my room and took out my phone to call Lisa. On the third ring, she picked up the phone.

"Hello? Willow?" she asked with an excited voice.

"Hey Lisa" I replied as I stacked few pillows on the headboard of the bed and moved to lie down comfortably.

"Sorry, I couldn't come and visit you today. My brother has come from Australia, so I had to be with my family" she said with a regretful voice.

"It's okay. I understand, spend a good time with your family. When you are free, we can meet" I said as she sighed with relief from the other side.

"Okay, so how are you feeling right now? Are you feeling any pain?" she asked with concern.

I sighed and replied," I am fine. I just feel bored and cooped up at home. I have so many classes, assignments, and exams pending, and just thinking about it is making me want to throw myself off this building".

She chuckled and said," Why am I here then? I will help you with everything, don't worry. Next time we meet I will get you all the notes".

"I know that.........I have something to tell you" I told her hesitating on whether to tell her or not. What if I am overanalyzing the matter? Anyway, I decided to tell her.

"My brother and sister have changed a lot. Suddenly my sister is wearing makeup and my brother for the first time yelled at me" I said letting out a deep sigh.

"OMG! I forgot to tell you something. I visited the hospital multiple times after you woke up, but your sister restricted me from seeing you. Maybe they were having tight security............ I don't know, but it seemed weird to me. I told her to inform me once you came home and today morning, she sent me the message" she told as I heard some shuffling noises on her side.

"Hey Willow, I need to go, my brother is calling. We will catch up later. Bye!" I told her bye and kept the phone down.

I was thinking about what Lisa said about my sister. Maybe this accident was caused by some rivals of my parents or siblings? That's why they were being so strict? Hmm, that might be the reason.

Since I didn't have any work to do, I decided to take a nap and give some rest to my tired body.

.

When I woke up the room was dark and I could hear the sound of laughter from downstairs. I got up and rubbed the sleep away from my eyes and pushed the covers off me. I freshened up and went downstairs, only to see my brother sitting in front of the TV and laughing loudly.

When he saw me coming down, he immediately changed to a news channel. 'What's wrong with him?' I thought to myself and walked towards the couch and sat beside him.

"Hey, you're home early? It's only 7 PM, usually, you would be back at 10 PM right?" I asked him as I made myself comfortable on the couch and watched the breaking news on the TV.

“Ah, I finished my work early today so I thought of coming home to take a rest. So did you sleep well?” he asked while he got up from the couch to go to the kitchen.

I turned towards him and replied,” Yes, I feel much better than today morning”.

I was about to ask him about Lisa’s visit to the hospital, but I stopped when my brother’s phone rang. I picked up the phone and saw the caller ID which read ‘Amelia’. Just as I was about to accept the call, the phone was snatched from my hands.

When I looked up at my brother, shocked by his rude actions, he said, “Never touch my phone” and stormed towards his room.

I sat there on the couch stunned by his actions. I have always used his phone and he has never objected even once. Today I wasn’t even snooping through his phone, I was just about to pick up our sister’s call. I felt so hurt by his actions. I always thought my brother loves me, but today I feel I was wrong all this time.

Or maybe he sees me as a burden now? That’s why he is treating me like this? What did I do to deserve such treatment?

I ran to my room with tears streaming down my face and negative thoughts plaguing my mind. I fell on my bed and curled into a ball crying to my heart’s content. I could feel my eyes trying to shut down and pull me to sleep.

Tomorrow when I wake up, I hope this is all just a nightmare.

...

I woke up startled when a thunder crackled in the skies. I pulled my covers off my legs and got down from the bed to close the windows. The rainwater had soaked the edges of the carpet. The room was pretty dark and I could only see the outlines of the objects in my room. I went and switched on the light and looked at the time, it read 5:30 AM. Since I woke up so soon, I didn't know what to do, so I again went to bed to take a nap.

I woke up and squinted my eyes as I could feel the brightness of the light sting my eyes. I saw that I had forgotten to switch off the lights and when I looked out of the window, it was still raining heavily. I looked at the time and it read 9 AM, so I stood up from the bed to do my morning routine. Once I finished dressing up, I went downstairs, hoping I don't meet my brother. I am still upset with him and I don't feel like talking to him.

As I was going down, I realized no one called me for dinner. I was really hungry and when I reached the hall no one was there, so I went to the kitchen straight to make some toast. The house was very silent and I realized everyone left for work, even my sister didn't come up to wake me up.

When I was about to open the fridge, I saw a sticky note posted on it by my mother. It read she was going shopping and will be back by lunch, at least my mother cared enough to write a note.

I sat at the dining table and ate my toasts while looking at the rain splattering on the windows. My mood was as gloomy as the weather. Cooped up at home while not being cared for by your loved ones is awful. As I finished eating, I washed my plates and kept them in racks. I went and sat on the couch to watch TV. I switched on the TV and flipped through the channels until I stopped at a particular news channel.

"Amelia Turner, a well-known businesswoman, has announced her engagement with her boyfriend of 5 months, who is the CEO of the chain of Hotels and Resorts Goldeneye, Mr. Jack Carter," the reporter said while they showed photos of my sister and her boyfriend standing together and waving at the cameras.

I was shocked as I saw the news. How come my sister never told me about this? Do my parents and brother know? Of course, they would have known. She has known him for only five months and she has already announced engagement? Isn't it too early? Such questions were running through my mind.

The news ended and the next news talked about charred bodies being discovered in the forests. While I was looking at my phone, thinking if I should call my sister, the door opened and my mom came in with bags from Gucci and Chanel.

The moment she looked up at me, she was surprised.

"Hey darling, you are awake already? Did you have your breakfast?" she asked as she removed her cooling glasses and kept the bags on the couch. I nodded with a small smile while she sat beside me and caressed my head while looking at the news that was running on the TV.

"You're watching the news? I assume you must have seen about your sister's engagement then?" she asked as made herself comfortable on the couch and looked at me.

"Yes, mom, what is even going on? Out of the blue, she announces her engagement with someone she has known only for five months? That's just ridiculous" I told her as I scoffed in disbelief.

My mother's face transformed into one of anger.

"Mind your words, young lady. You're talking about your sister. It's her life, her decisions. You don't have any right to comment upon it, understood? Focus on getting better and studying" she told with a stern and angry voice and took her bags as she stormed off to her room.

I was stunned by my mom's outburst. Why did she get so worked up over what I said? I was just shocked about my sister's sudden decision, so I expressed my feelings to her. Is it so wrong? As someone who cares about her, can't I question?

I could feel my eyes burning from the unshed tears. I closed my eyes and wiped the tears that slid down my cheeks. In the six months, I have become unwanted to my family, and a burden to them. I should probably stop interfering in matters pertaining to the family and focus on my life.

I switched off the TV and went up to my room to be alone because I need to learn to be alone when my family abandons me.

•

When I woke up, the room was pitch dark. I got up and pushed the covers away and switched on my phone that was kept on the side table to look at the time, it read 9 PM.

I went and freshened up to go down and have something since my stomach was making noises. When I went down, I saw my family sitting in the hall and laughing while watching the TV. I felt so alone at that point, but I didn't want to show that I was affected, so I went straight to the kitchen, to cook some pasta for myself. As I was waiting for the water to boil my sister came to the kitchen.

"Willow, what are you doing? Do you need any help?" my sister asked as she came and stood beside me.

"No need" I replied without looking at her. I could feel her gaze on the side of my face, but I refused to turn and look at her.

"Are you angry with me?" she asked with hesitancy.

By the time the water had boiled so I added the pasta into the water and looked at her.

"Why would I be angry at you? I just want to cook on my own that's it" I replied with a small fake smile and looked at the pasta getting cooked.

She sighed and mumbled an okay and went back to the couch and sat beside our brother. Once I cooked the pasta, I took a plate and some iced tea in a tray to take it upstairs and eat. Just when I was about to walk towards the stairs, my brother came running while my sister followed him giggling, and he pushed me to the side and the tray fell and the food spilled on the floor.

This time I let the tears fall and my anger shot up like a volcano. I looked at my brother with red-rimmed eyes, but before I can explode, he shouted at me.

"ARE YOU OUT OF YOUR MIND? CAN'T YOU SEE THAT I'M COMING NEAR THE STAIRS? You should be careful since you are the one holding the food tray" he told with an angered voice

I looked at him with disbelief. Is he seriously blaming me for his carelessness?

I scoffed and replied," I can't believe how ridiculous you have become. You were the one running around blindly and then you blame me? Wow! I am speechless".

I let out all my anger and didn't hold back. But his next reply broke my heart completely.

"Princess, get this into your mind. You have been getting onto my nerves since you recovered and I am getting fed up with you. So please kindly fuck off" he replied with such hate and I was stunned.

Before he could storm off, I held his hand and stopped him to ask one last question that has been plaguing my mind.

"So, all this time I was unwanted and you faked your love for me?" I asked with tears spilling from my eyes without any stop.

Something unreadable flashed across his eyes and his eyes darkened as he replied, "Yes, finally your pea-sized brain could understand this. Now can you leave my hand?".

I left his hand and he stormed to his room while my sister and parents just stood by watching whatever happened with sympathetic faces, neither of them coming forward to defend me.

I smiled at my pathetic self and went upstairs and closed the door. Today I understood my place in the family and the importance I hold. Tomorrow I have to leave this place if I need to retain my self-respect.

...

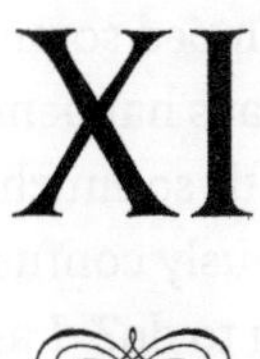

I woke up to a severe headache as if someone was drilling into my head, the pain worsened when I tried to get up. I lied down again and let myself calm down and slowly got up and sat on the bed. I drank some water and calmed myself down, while the pain slowly subsided leaving behind a numbing pain. I got up from the bed and went to get refreshed. I thought of having my breakfast and then take my bags and go to Lisa's home temporarily until I can find a place for myself. I had texted her yesterday night if I could come over and stay for a few days and she agreed happily since it's been a long time since we met.

Once dressed, I took my mobile and went downstairs to get some breakfast. As soon as I reached the bottom of the stairs, I suddenly felt dizzy and I grabbed the handles of the stairs to stabilize myself. My brother and parents who were sitting on the couch immediately looked at me and rushed towards my side.

My brother had a worried face and asked me, "Are you okay Willow?"

My parents also had worried faces and looked at me expecting an answer. Once I felt okay, I simply nodded, confused about their sudden behavior change. My brother took me to the couch and made me sit, as he went to get a glass of water for me.

I took the glass and sipped some water, to calm myself. I couldn't understand what's happening right now. Yesterday he was yelling at me with so much hatred and today he is caring for me, I am seriously confused.

"What are you trying to do?" I asked him with a serious voice and he looked a bit taken aback.

"What do you mean Willow? I am taking care of you" he said with an obvious and surprised voice. He was about to touch my shoulder when I got up from the couch and stood away from him.

"Do not touch me. Yesterday you were yelling at me and admitted that I am a burden and today you are acting as if you care about me. Wow! I am impressed with your acting. I know your true form, so you can drop your act" I said harshly and was about to go to the kitchen when my mom spoke.

"Willow! What the hell are you talking about? Yesterday nothing of that sort happened. How can you speak to your brother like that? She asked with anger laced in her voice. My brother was standing like a statue shocked by my accusations.

"Mom, please, you were present here when he pushed me while running away from Amelia. And when I yelled at him for pushing me and spilling my food, he told such hurtful words to me. After seeing him act like that, how can you support him?"

"What are you even talking about? I was not at home yesterday night, I was at the company since I had a lot of work to do. Whatever you are talking about never happened."

He said in a desperate voice and what confused me more was my mom and dad were nodding their heads indicating whatever he is saying was true.

"Do you think I am fabricating lies? I remember very well that this incident happened yesterday. Ok, if not, tell me what I was doing yesterday?" I asked them as I folded my hands against my chest and looked at my brother and mother.

"You were not well and slept the whole day yesterday. Today morning when you woke up did you have a headache?" my father asked me and I was shocked. How did he know that I had a headache?

"H-How do you know that?" I asked him still shocked.

"It is the side effect of the medicine. I guess you must have dreamt about everything that happened."

As I stood there confused by their accounts of what happened yesterday, I remembered I packed my bags yesterday and also texted Lisa about me coming over. I immediately took my phone that was on the couch and checked for the messages, but my message to Lisa wasn't there.

How is that possible? I did send the text yesterday. The last option I had left was to check for my luggage. I ran upstairs to my room and found no luggage near the window, where I had left it the night before. I could feel my head pounding again and before I could move another step, I fell and the next thing I met was darkness.

•••

I could hear someone talking in the background. I slowly tried to open my eyes and looked at the ceiling and blinked my eyes a few times. I saw my sister sitting by my bedside and talking to someone on her phone. When she saw me moving a bit and awake, she immediately cut the call and leaned towards me.

"Willow, are you okay? How is your head?" she asked with a worried tone.

"I am okay," I told her as I got up and moved myself to the headboard of the bed.

"Why are you here? I asked as I looked at her straight.

"What do you mean? I am here to take care of you" she told as she tried to keep her hand on my shoulder.

I moved away slightly and chuckled.

"You don't need to act as if you care because if you had cared for me, you would have talked about your fiancé to me," I told her as I looked away from her.

She looked at me incredulously.

"Willow, have you forgotten? I did tell you about him before I announced the engagement" she told me in disbelief.

"What? Are you kidding me? If you had told me I would remember. Even yesterday, my brother and parents pointed out an incident that happened as never happened. I very well remember it happened, but there was no proof to show it happened. I feel like I'm losing my mind" I told her as tears collected in the corner of my eyes due to the frustration.

"Willow, I am sorry you're going through this, but you need to trust us. The incidents that you think did happen, never happened and the things you think never happened, have happened" she told as she looked at me with sympathy.

"I want to be alone," I told her as I looked at the window.

She tried to say something but I refused to listen and she slowly got up to go out of the room. Once she was out of the room, I looked at the side table to take my phone, but I saw another phone on the table. The phone belonged to Amelia, my sister. I picked up her phone to give it back to her, when a message popped up on the screen, that turned my blood cold.

'Are you giving her the medicines properly? Give it regularly for results. Once the headache increases bring her to me.'

I was shocked to read the message. What does this mean? Is she trying to worsen my headache? But why would she do that? Something is wrong.

I immediately went to freshen up and when I came out, I saw she still hasn't come to pick up her phone. That's weird. She always has her phone in her hand.

I took both our phones and went down slowly as I heard my brother and father talking. I tiptoed and hid and listened to what they were talking about.

"Son, how is the plan going on?

"It's going perfectly. We just need to monitor her medicine intake and once she reaches the state we require, we can eliminate her" my brother said.

I gasped silently hearing whatever they were talking about. Why does my family want to eliminate me? What is even happening around me?

Just before my father could utter a word, Amelia's phone rang distracting my brother and father. I immediately acted as if I was coming down the stairs.

I looked at my brother and father, who looked at me and smiled, I returned their smile and searched for Amelia.

"Dad, where is Amelia?" I asked him.

Before he could Amelia came from her room, fresh after her shower.

"Oh sorry, I forgot my phone in your room," she said in a panicked tone and snatched the mobile from my hands to answer the call. She picked up the call and went to her room and closed the door.

I looked at my brother and father, who looked a bit nervous.

"Willow, did Amelia get any calls or messages from her fiancé?" my brother asked as he looked at me trying to hide his nervousness.

I remembered the message from my doctor and I looked at him with furrowed eyebrows.

"No, she didn't get any calls, I don't know about the messages" I replied.

"Oh ok," my brother said with a small smile.

I smiled and went to the kitchen with so many thoughts plaguing my mind.

I need to figure out what they are planning, I thought to myself.

I poured myself some juice and toasted bread for breakfast. Just before I could take a bite, I received a call from Lisa.

"Hey, Lisa! How are you?" I asked her with an excited tone.

"I am good. How about you?" she asked me

"Yeah, I'm good. I have something important to talk about" I replied.

"Same here, can we meet? It's about your parents" she asked me with an urgent tone.

I furrowed my eyebrows at her tone and tensed when she talked about my parents.

I immediately replied "Sure. What time and where?"

"How about in an hour at the new café?"

"Okay. We will meet there" I told her as she cut the call.

Thinking about what urgent matter she wanted to say, I wore a black hoodie and a pair of black jeans and tied my hair into a ponytail. I took my purse and was about to leave my home when my mother came in front of me.

"Where are you going?" she asked me with curiosity.

"I am going to meet Lisa," I told her and was about to move, but she blocked my way again.

"For what purpose are you meeting her?" she asked me with a raised eyebrow.

"Mom, why are you screwing me with questions? I am meeting her to update myself on my studies. So please stop questioning and move out of my way" I said and pushed past her shoulders to go outside.

I walked to the nearest bus stop to take a bus to the café. My mom has never cared about where I go and what I do, but suddenly today she is concerned about my activities. Maybe she isn't concerned but keeping an eye on my activities? Just the thought of it brought shivers down my spine.

After 15 minutes of bus ride, I arrived at the café. Once I went inside, I searched for Lisa, but she was nowhere to be seen. Maybe she is late, I thought to myself and sat by a secluded table and decided to wait for her.

It's been an hour and still no sign of her. I called her multiple times but her phone kept ringing. I decided to try calling her for the last time, but this time, the phone was switched off. This made me paranoid since she never switches off her phone. What if something happened to her? I have no way of contacting her. I don't even know her address.

I decided to go home and wait until she contacts me. I reached home after 30 minutes and sat on the couch tired. I went to the kitchen to drink some water and turned to go upstairs to my room when I saw three drops of blood near my brother's room. The immediate thought that he must have been hurt flashed across my mind. I worriedly went near his room to open the door, when I heard him speaking to someone,

"Amelia, that girl has been eliminated," he told her and cut the call.

I stood frozen hearing whatever came out of his mouth. When I heard him getting up, I immediately ran upstairs and closed my door without making any sound. Hot tears fell down my cheeks because somehow, I realized that the girl, they were talking about is Lisa.

Who am I even living with? Do I even know my own family? Why do I feel like they are strangers?

...

XIII

I washed my face with cold water and dabbed my face with a towel. My eyes were red and puffy from all the crying. I can't let them know that I know about their deeds. I have to be careful if I need to be alive. I took a deep breath and once my face looked normal and not like I bawled my eyes out, I went down taking my phone. It was already five pm.

Once I reached the hall, I saw my father and mother getting ready to go somewhere. Once my mother saw me, she smiled at me and came towards me.

"How are you feeling Willow? Is your headache still there?" she asked me with a concerned face. I didn't know if it was a real or fake concern.

"I'm feeling good mom" I mumbled and went to the kitchen to drink some water. I felt nervous to even look at their faces, the fear of them finding out I know about them killing Lisa is too much.

"Hey Willow" my sister came to the kitchen to drink water. She saw me and smiled whereas I gave a fake smile. I don't think it would be possible for me to be real towards them.

My mother came to the kitchen and asked Amelia.

"Dear, get ready soon. The party starts in about two hours, you should look gorgeous" she said with a fond smile on her face. I didn't understand what party they were talking about. Seeing my confused face my sister turned my face towards her.

"Willow, today we are keeping a party for the merging of my company and my fiancé's company. So, get dolled up quickly since the party is in about two hours" she said with a smile on her face.

What the hell? Seriously? They didn't even tell me that they are hosting a party and told me just two hours before? What kind of lunacy is this? I mentally scoffed as I finished drinking the remaining water.

I nodded and was about to go to my room when my mom asked me a question that made me burn from inside.

"How did the meeting with Lisa yesterday go, dear? How is she?" she asked with a sweet fake smile adorned on her face.

I lost control of my emotions and whirled around to look at her with a fire burning in my eyes. The moment our eyes met she looked a bit taken aback. But before I could lash out at her, my brother interrupted the conversation by entering the kitchen.

"Mom, we need to be there in an hour, the guests will start arriving," he said facing mom while avoiding me. At that moment I regained control over my emotions and left the kitchen to go and get ready for the party, which I was least interested in visiting.

I wore the dress my brother bought for my birthday last year, which had golden shiny stones decorating the neck and bottom of the dress and had a low neck with full sleeves. I put on some light makeup giving a golden glow to my face. I took my golden clutch and put my phone inside.

I dolled up myself in golden color, from the clip on my hair to the heels on my feet.

It was five-thirty pm by the time I got ready and went down, where my mother and sister were waiting for me. Once they saw me, they gushed at how pretty I looked and ushered me to get into the car as we were getting late.

We got into the car and the driver drove off to the event, which was happening at Goldeneye Hotel, owned by Jack Carter, my sister's fiancé. Today I am planning to expose my family for killing Lisa and also planning to kill me. This is the best chance to confront and expose them to the world. Yes, I dearly loved them as my family, but all along they were only faking it and my brother has humiliated me multiple times, showing me that I am no one to him. The only thing that always confuses me is, how can someone change this much in six months? As I was in deep thoughts, I realized that we reached the Hotel. They escorted us inside the Hotel as I walked beside my sister wearing a smile on my face for the reporters and photographers clicking our pictures. The flashes and noisy questions were too much and I felt like running away from there and going back to the safety of my home. This is why I avoided public gatherings.

We entered the spacious hall decorated in Greek style with huge chandeliers decorating the ceiling, with gorgeous women and handsome men standing in groups sipping wine. Once we entered the hall, again flashes filled the hall and people started cheering for Amelia, while raising their wine glasses.

There was a stage with a projector and a big screen, while the garden, which was located at the end of the hall, had a buffet spread and tables put out on the lush green grass.

I stood along with my mom and sister while we talked with other important business people. Then my sister gripped my wrist and pulled me towards a man who was tall, lean and had blonde hair which was gelled up, adorned in a white suit with chocolate brown eyes and a perfectly sculpted face.

"Willow, this is my fiancé, Jack. I am sure you must have seen him on TV" she said while giggling and pecking on his cheeks while blushing. I smiled at him and said hello while shaking his hands.

The lights slowly dimmed and spotlights for the stage glowed brightly as Mr. Carter, father of Jack Carter, came up to the stage with a wide smile. He was stout and was in his 60s.

"Good evening ladies and gentlemen, I welcome you to this fabulous evening to celebrate the partnership of the Turner and Carter family, in both business and family relationship," he said with a proud smile as everyone was cheering and applauding.

"I invite my precious son and his fiancé to give a talk on their beautiful relationship," he said while clapping and cheering for them to come on the stage. I was looking at the stage with a bored look on my face.

As I was looking around the hall, I saw my brother standing in a corner and talking to someone very seriously. He cut the call angrily and went to the corridor which had a metal plate showing the direction to the restroom. I slowly escaped from the crowd and went behind my brother without making any sound. The corridor was empty with pastel yellow lights illuminating the corridor. Two milky pine doors read male and female, as I was about to enter the male door, I heard my brother's voice at the end of the corridor. He was entering the door at the end of the corridor without closing the door. He kept his phone and removed his coat and went to the restroom. Immediately I tiptoed into the room and took his phone and unlocked it. I searched for his messages and found a message which contained the details of Lisa along with her photo. Then below the message, there was another message sent by my brother which read 'You know what to do'.

Before I could screenshot it and send it to my phone, the bathroom door opened and my brother stepped out looking at me with a smirk.

"Look at the curious cat who sneaked into my room," he said as he slowly walked towards me. He took the phone out of my hand and saw what I was doing on his phone. His face changed into an unreadable expression and suddenly glared at me intensely.

"What are you doing with my phone?" he asked while keeping his phone in his pocket.

This was my chance to confront him about Lisa.

"Why do you have Lisa's details?" I asked him while glaring at him.

He looked at me with a confused look and furrowed eyebrows.

"Umm, who is Lisa?" he asked me innocently.

I felt the rage erupt inside me like a volcano. I stormed towards him and gripped his collar tightly.

"WHAT THE HECK IS WRONG WITH YOU? ARE YOU OUT OF YOUR FUCKING MIND? YOU ARE THE ONE WHO KILLED MY FRIEND LISA" I screamed at him with tears rolling down my face. He looked at me with a blank expression while pushing me backward.

"Willow I think you are delusional. You have imaginary friends, I guess. Since when?" he said as he chuckled and took the coat that was on the bed and started to move towards the door. I thought I could control the situation but now it was going out of hand. I had to do something and expose him. I immediately went towards him and snatched the phone that was in his right hand. He was surprised by my sudden action and tried to grab his phone away from me, but before that, I ran away from the room towards the hall.

The heels were killing my feet, but I refused to stop and ran towards the hall. This is my chance to expose him. I went near the projector and opened the phone to connect it to the projector and show the text messages. I got onto the stage and shouted so that I can get everyone's attention. The people who were standing in small groups, talking and laughing were startled by my sudden loud voice. All the people gathered in the hall had their attention on me.

"Hello everyone, I have something important to say," I said nervously and took a deep breath. Am I doing this right? I should expose him right or should I keep it a secret? What if no one believes me? Such doubts and fears started consuming me and I started panicking. But I have already come on the stage and started talking, backing out now will look foolish. No matter what, I have to continue what I came for, I said to myself and gripped the mike tightly until my knuckles turned white.

•

Back in the hotel room, Mark stood stunned as Willow ran out of the room with his phone. He chuckled to himself and took the other phone from his side pocket and called someone.

"Hey! Emergency. You know what to do" he said and cut the call with a smirk on his face.

"My poor Willow, how stupid you are," he said to no one and started laughing crazily.

Willow looked at the gathering, who were curious to know what she was about to say.

"My brother killed my best friend, Lisa." The moment I said this, I heard a few gasps and the crowd started murmuring between themselves. From the end of the hall, I saw my parents and sister storming towards me with fury etched on their faces. My sister came on the stage and tried to pull me off the stage gently while whispering in my ear.

"Willow enough of your bullshit. What is wrong with you? Are you trying to tarnish our family name?" she asked me with rage dripping from her voice. I looked at her with anger and shouted.

"Oh please, I thought our family is great and the best but now I know you guys are just filth. On one side not only did you murder my best friend but you guys are also planning to kill me. I know about your evil plans. I am ashamed to call you guys my family." I spat on her face and turned towards a voice from the crowd.

"Ms. Willow, I understand you want to expose the misdeeds of your family, but if you want people to believe you need proof," a media person from the crowd told and the others also nodded in response and started asking for proof.

"Yes, I have the proof. I can show you right now" I said and took out my brother's phone. Just when I was about to unlock the phone, I saw my brother at the end of the hall looking at me with a smirk. And that smirk scared me. I gulped in fear and opened the text messages. I opened the chat in which he had sent her profile and scrolled up to the particular message I wanted. But when I scrolled through the text messages, I was shocked. The message about Lisa wasn't there, it had disappeared. I swear to God, that I saw the message, then how come it disappeared.

Every one started murmuring among them and I could feel fear and panic clawing against my throat. I wanted to disappear, I felt like puking, I wanted to shout to the crowd that my brother did something to the text messages, but I did none of them. I stood frozen looking at my brother who started walking towards the stage with a sad and innocent face. He came up to the stage and took the mike from my hand, while I kept staring at him.

"I am sorry for the inconvenience caused by my dear sister. As you guys know she has been hallucinating and having delusions since she recovered from the accidents. This is one of her episodes. Please forgive us for her behavior" he told and switched off the mike while having an iron grip on my hand he pulled me off the stage. The guests were murmuring about my mental state and saying that I should receive psychiatric care. I didn't fight my brother's hold and let him drag me. My dumb self thought I could fight against such big people and expose them. Oh, how wrong I was.

If I had been a little bit stronger, I would have saved myself; If I had been a little bit smarter, I would have found out the reality of my family.

...

My brother dragged me into our car, followed by my parents. My sister stayed behind to send off the guests. I just looked out of the window while my mom was cursing and shouting at me for ruining the image and reputation of the family. Once we entered the hall, I dropped my heels and walked towards the couch, and sat on it.

My brother came and threw his phone on the couch and pulled me up to a standing position. I didn't look at him and kept staring at the wall opposite me. He gripped my jaw harshly and made me face him.

"ARE YOU OUT OF YOUR FUCKING MIND? WHAT KIND OF SHIT WERE YOU TRYING TO PULL THERE?" he asked with gritted teeth.

"Wow, this is the first time I have heard you swear so much in one sentence," I said sarcastically, as I looked straight into his eyes.

He scoffed and pushed me back as I stumbled on the carpet. I glared at him with tears in my eyes. My brother always says that he hates to see tears in my eyes, but now he looked at me with so much hatred and didn't care about my tears. I could feel intense rage erupt inside me as I kept seeing him.

I stormed towards him and pushed him back as his back hit the wall.

"WHAT DID YOU DO TO LISA? I KNOW YOU KILLED HER. DON'T TRY TO FOOL ME BY SAYING SHE IS MY IMAGINARY FRIEND" I shouted at him with tears streaming down my face.

He scoffed and pushed himself away from the wall and came closer to me.

"First prove Lisa is real," he said and went and sat on the couch as my parents glared at me with so much hatred and stormed towards their room. I wiped my tears and turned towards my brother sitting on the couch.

"Okay I will prove it to you right now," I said and lifted my gown so that I don't trip and fall face-first on the stairs. I went into my room and took the box which had my albums and photos. I took the yearbook and rushed downstairs and gave it to my brother. He moved a bit from the place he was previously sitting and pulled me down beside him.

"Open and show her photo," he said and started scrolling through his phone.

I flipped through the pages and came to the page where the student's name starting with L was located. I searched for Lisa's name but I couldn't find it. How is that possible? I panicked and immediately searched the same page again, then the whole yearbook but she wasn't there. My brother looked at me with raised eyebrows and smirked.

"Poor girl, you didn't find your Lisa?" he mocked me while chuckled and said, "I told you right she is your imaginary friend," he said and got up from the couch and walked to his room, and slammed the door.

The yearbook in my hand fell and I stood there like a lifeless doll. What is happening around me? Is Lisa not real? Was I the only one imagining her? No, that can't be true.

He is trying to manipulate me by inserting such thoughts. But if she is real, why is she not present in the yearbook? I gripped my hair and screamed as I let out my frustrations. I wanted to cry but the tears refused to come out. Feeling exhausted by the onslaught of emotions, I took the yearbook that was on the floor and turned to go upstairs, when the front door slammed upon and my sister stormed in. The moment she saw me, she came and slapped me right across my face. I kept my hand on the throbbing cheek and looked at her without any emotions.

"Are you happy now? Why did you have to spoil my day? How dare you spoil our parents' reputation? She screamed as she gripped my shoulders.

Hearing the voice of my sister my parents and brother came out. My father came and pulled my sister away from me.

"Amelia, that's enough. All that happened today was due to her sickness. After the accident you know very well, she has been hallucinating and having delusions, which has also been informed to the crowd today. So don't worry, tomorrow we will take her to the doctor and probably get a psychiatric consultation" he told calmly and signaled my brother to take my sister away.

I looked at my father with tears in my eyes.

"Dad, y-you think I am i-insane?" I asked him as I felt everything around me crumbling down.

"Yes, you need psychiatric help," he said with an emotionless face. I laughed at his statement and looked at him with fury in my eyes.

"Oh, so I guess the medicines you guys gave me worked its magic?" I asked and glared at my parents who had shocked faces and brother and sister stopped in their steps.

"So now, you guys can send me away and eliminate me from your lives? Wasn't that your plan brother?" I asked as he turned around and looked at me with a slight shock on his face but immediately masked it with an unreadable expression.

"The family I knew before used to care for me and love me so much, but after the accident, the same family is treating me like a burden. Maybe you guys acted fake all these years and now you decided to show me your true colors?" I asked looking at my parents.

"Mom, since you are sending me away, fulfill your promise," I said and looked at my mother. She stood there looking at me confusedly.

"Mom, you promised me you would give it, the day I leave this house. Since I am going to leave, give it to me, at least it will act as a remembrance of those who loved me truly." I said and looked expectantly at my mother.

"Mom, why are you looking so cluelessly? You promised before you left for your work trip"

My mom stood there nervously while fiddling with her fingers.

"What? You don't want to give me? You even told me it is Grandma's last wish. You promised her."

My brother tried to signal something to my father and I felt suspicious.

"What is going on here? Mom, tell me what was Grandma's last wish?" I asked as I looked at her with suspicion.

"You are the only one who knows her last wish," I said and took a step forward.

I have never seen my mother nervous and she loves her mother-in-law so much. Both of them had a great bond, like a mother and daughter. When she died, my mom was so shocked and it took her months to get back to normal. When grandma told her last wish, she told me she would give the family ring to me when I leave home.

"Mom answer me!" I shout but she stood there silently watching me without any expression and it was creeping me out. My father, mother, brother, and sister were standing without any expression, and for the first time, I feared my family.

"What is wrong with you all? Why are you guys acting like strangers? I shouted in fear and nervousness.

Then slowly all of them smiled at me widely which creeped me out and my brother said, "Oops, she found out."

...

I don't know why but the first instinct was to run towards the door, but before I could reach it, my brother pulled me and locked the door.

"Princess, where are you running to?" he asked with an evil smirk on his face.

"LEAVE ME ALONE" I shouted and tried to wiggle myself out of his hold.

He dragged me to the couch, pushed me on it, and walked and stood with the others.

"What is going on? Why are you guys acting like this?" I asked with a trembling voice.

All of them started laughing crazily as I sat there terrified and tears streaming down my face.

"My poor sister, we are not your family," my sister said as she came and sat by my side.

"W-What? I asked still unable to comprehend.

My brother sighed as he got chairs for his parents and as well as for himself. Once he sat down, he looked at me with a smirk.

"We killed your family by burning them alive. We are doppelgängers of your family, princess."

What? Doppelgängers? I felt confused, angry, sad, and didn't know what to feel. How come I didn't see they are different from my family?

"Stop thinking so hard princess. I will explain everything" Mark, my so-called brother said.

"Do you remember the day you saw the news about Amelia's engagement? If you remember you were also seeing another news about four charred bodies found in a forest? Does it strike anything?" my mother asked as she looked at me with an amused expression.

News about four charred bo-? Oh yeah, I remember the news. But why is she suddenly talking about it? Does she mean that those bodies belong to my family?

"Yes, I remember," I said hesitantly praying those bodies are not my family.

"Oh princess, they are your family. We killed them a month after you went into a coma" Mark said while smiling at me.

My hands were trembling due to the sudden news and I felt dizzy. Have I been living with strangers and also killers all these months? I looked at Mark with tears in my eyes.

"We have been planning this for years. Since we look identical to your family and them being popular gave us an amazing idea. We decided to replace your family. I kept an eye on your family without anyone's notice. That day when you were in the café with your friend Lisa, I was the one standing at the end of the forest and watching you. And by the way" he chuckled as he continued, "Your friend Lisa is real, not a figment of your imagination. She was about to ruin our years of hard work, so I had no other way, but to eliminate her. After we had gathered enough information about your family, we were thinking about how to take the place of your family. And the right opportunity presented itself when your parents came back from their long work trip. Since you don't have a doppelgänger, we decided to eliminate you. So, on the day you were supposed to meet your parents, we arranged an accident to take place. But unfortunately, you didn't die on the spot as we expected but went into a coma. We didn't know when you would wake up, so we had to do everything before you wake up. One month after you went into a coma, we killed your family and started adjusting as the Turner Family. We made sure you would never doubt us when you wake up, so we perfected the way we behave, months before you woke up" he said and went to the kitchen to drink water.

"You did notice some differences in us, but thankfully you didn't become suspicious. My brother doesn't know to cook whereas your brother knew. Your sister loves light makeup whereas I love heavy makeup. Your mom doesn't spend too much money on expensive things whereas my mom spent a lot on expensive stuff. I think your gears are turning now" she said and chuckled while looking at me thinking back to the events.

Oh my god! How didn't I notice all this? I have been living in a lie all these months. My head was hurting and my throat was aching due to suppressing my tears. The family that I loved with every fiber of my being is no more? I don't have anyone in this world. I sobbed silently while gripping the arms of the couch. I had one last question I wanted to ask them. I controlled my tears and wiped them before looking at Mark who came back after drinking water.

"Can I ask a question? I asked with a hoarse voice from all the crying.

"Yeah sure," he said and focusing on me.

"Why? Why are you doing all this?" I asked as more tears rolled down my face.

"I thought you are smart, princess. By now, you must know the reason" he said and looked at me with raised eyebrows.

"Money?" I mumbled hesitantly.

"What? Can you speak louder?" he asked with an amused expression

"Money," I told him a bit louder after clearing my throat.

"Yes, perfect. Money is the reason we killed your parents and took over their place"

Suddenly I felt extreme anger bubbling inside of me. I stood up from the couch and slapped him right across his face. The force was extreme as my palm started to burn. His face which went to the other side slowly turned and looked at me with shock and kept his palm on his throbbing cheek. Others were extremely shocked, to the point where they looked frozen.

"WHAT THE FUCK IS WRONG WITH YOU? YOU DID ALL THIS FOR SOME MONEY? YOU KILLED MY FAMILY, ALL FOR THIS STUPID MONEY?" I shouted at him completely consumed by anger.

I scoffed and looked at him, "If you wanted money, you could have asked my parents, they would have thrown some at your face" I said with a venom-filled voice.

He pushed back by my shoulders onto the coffee table and stood up from his chair. He was provoked by my words and was enraged.

"SHUT UP! You were born and brought up in money, so what do you know about money? DO you know its value? Do you know what is poverty? What it feels like to be poor without a single penny for even food? We had to struggle for one meal a day, for good clothes, for a decent place to stay. But you had all the luxuries, got what you wanted, never faced financial difficulties, so don't talk about money. You don't have the fucking right. Since we had the same face as your family, we had to disguise ourselves, so that no one would identify us. We couldn't live normally" he spat on my face with so much venom, that I was taken aback by his hatred.

"We were in a dilemma of whether to keep you alive or kill you. Now, what should I do with you? He asked as he took a step forward.

"Kill me," I told without any second thought. In a world where I have no one, what's the point in living?

"Ah, that was so easy. Hmm......how about no? Since you chose to die, I will choose the other option? What do you guys say?" he asked the others and they all nodded with a creepy smile on their faces.

As he was looking at them for confirmation, I immediately ran towards the door to escape. But before I could reach the handle of the door, Mark grabbed me by my waist and pulled me back as he leaned in and whispered in my ears, "Nope, we are not letting you go princess" he said and chuckled evilly.

...

XVI

I tried to wiggle out of his iron grip by kicking him in his legs and even tried to butt heads with him, but it was of no use. He dragged me towards the stairs, to my room, and pushed me inside, disregarding my screams. He secured the window with digital locks so that I won't be able to escape. Before closing the door, he threw me a water bottle and smiled as he said, "Have a happy stay, princess". He slammed the door with a 'bam' as I screamed at him to let me out, but he was already gone. I fell to the floor with tears sliding down my cheeks as I pulled my legs towards my chest and cried my heart out.

I miss my family so much..........I didn't even get to see them for the last time............ I didn't get to hug my parents.........Why is life so cruel to me? At a point, I could feel my eyes getting heavy as I blacked out on the carpeted floor.

I woke up to someone opening the door and I opened my eyes slightly. The moment I open my eyes I immediately shut them due to the sudden brightness. I saw my sister putting a plate of food and before closing the door she looked at me and said, "Eat well".

I looked at the time and it was 7 AM. My arm and neck were aching since I slept on the hard floor. I sat up and rotated my neck and arms to relieve the pain. I went and got refreshed and came to drink some water and looked at the food. I didn't have the appetite to eat, all I wanted to do was curl up on my bed and cry. I sat there staring at the wall when I realized that sitting like this is going to be of no help and I have to escape as soon as possible and report these doppelgängers to the police. I had to think of a quick way to get out from here. The remaining day I checked the existence of any possible ways of escape, but none existed. At night, again Amelia came to give the dinner and a bottle of water, right when she was about to go out, she got a call. She answered the call and her face became pale, without a second to waste she dashed out of the room, without closing the door.

I took this chance to run out of the room without making any noise. I peeped down at the hall and saw Mr. Turner sitting while watching the TV. I had to distract him somehow, so I took a pebble from the potted plants that were lined near the staircase and threw it towards the kitchen. The pebble smashed the glass jar which contained water and crashed to the floor. Due to the sudden sound, he immediately turned towards it and ran to the kitchen. The moment he got up, I dashed down the stairs and towards the door. Once I went out, I sprinted to the nearest police station, which took me about 10 minutes.

Once I reached the police station, I rushed inside breathing heavily. An officer was sitting in his chair and signing a few papers.

"Sir, I would like to register a complaint," I said as I went near him.

"Hmm......what is the complaint?" he asked as he looked at me with disinterest.

"My name is Willow Turner and- "he interrupted me and looked at me with wide eyes.

"You are from the Turner family? Oh my god, why didn't you tell me beforehand? Please take a seat" he said while getting up and pulling out the chair for me.

"Since you don't come out to the public much, I didn't know who you are. The latest news of you at the party was the one I saw, but your picture was blurred out" he explained with a nervous look.

"Sir, please help me out. My family is a group of doppelgängers. They not only killed my real family when I was in a coma but also killed my friend. They are acting as if they are the Turners. The four charred bodies that were discovered in the forest belong to my family." I said desperately with tearful eyes.

"Miss, what are you talking about? How is that even possible? He asked as he looked at me with disbelief.

"I know it is not easy to believe, but it's the truth. Please believe me. They even had me locked up in my room for a day" I said in a desperate tone.

"Do you have proof to back up your statement?" he asked me as he leaned forward on the table.

"No, I don't have any proof. But please believe me" I said as tears rolled down my face.

"I am sorry miss, but-," before he could complete his sentence his phone rang. He picked it up with a serious face and nodded to whatever the person said on the opposite side. He cut the call and looked at me.

"Miss, please wait here, let me see what I can do," he said and went to the other room in the building.

I was waiting for 15 minutes when I heard footsteps towards the room. The door opened and the person I least expected walked in along with the officer I was talking to.

He walked towards me and whispered in my ear.

"Hello princess, what a surprise?" he asked with an amused expression. I panicked and looked for something to defend myself. I saw the globe on the table and threw it at him. He dodged it successfully and stared at me with fake concern.

"Sir, these are the paper works for her admission into the psychiatric facility and her health reports. I am sorry for the inconvenience she has caused" Mark said and handed the files to the police officer.

"What the hell are you talking about? I am perfectly fine" I screamed at him.

Suddenly two people came inside and held my arms as they started dragged me out. Mark looked sad as they dragged me out and he was facing the police officer. What a good actor, I thought to myself.

"LEAVE ME ALONE! I AM PERFECTLY FINE. HE IS LYING" I cried and screamed at them, but my words were paid no attention. As they were taking me to the car, Mark smirked at me when no one saw.

When we reached the facility, I had completely calmed down, there was no point in fighting when you know you are not going to be believed. They made me sign a few papers and one of the attendants informed me that I would be spending my time here till I become alright. I nodded emotionlessly as they lead me to a locker room where I was given a change of clothes. Then they lead me down a long hallway which was lined up with rooms, in which patients resided. They took me to the room at the end of the hallway and let me in and closed the door. It was a small room which had a table and chair with a bed in the corner and an attached toilet. There was a window that had Crisscross grills to avoid patients escaping. I sat on the bed and looked out of the window, as I came to an understanding that my life will be spent in the psychiatric facility and I had no escape from it.

...

XVII

Epilogue

2 years later

Willow and her friend were sitting in the cafeteria and eating their food silently. A staff came and switched on the television and switched it to a news channel. The girl beside Willow was talking about something excitedly while Willow was silently listening to her and occasionally responding with a hum or a small smile.

"Hey Willow, today we are having a new admission," she said excitedly while picking up the toast and spreading some jam on it.

Before Willow could respond, the news running on the TV catches her attention.

"Yesterday night at around 9 PM, the Turner family was found brutally murdered in their home. There was no sign of a break-in, so police are assuming it must be someone known to the family. The crime scene was so gruesome, that few police officers couldn't stand the scene. The police are currently investigating the case and are in search of the perpetrator."

The newsreader finished the news and moved on to the next one. Willow looked at the TV in shock, not knowing whether to feel happy or sad. While she was trying to comprehend the news, she heard some chaos at the entrance of the cafeteria. She looked up but couldn't see who it was due to the people crowding around the person. She sighed and resumed eating when she heard footsteps stop near her table. Her friend beside her gasped loudly and this made Willow lookup. She was speechless and shocked when she saw the girl standing in front of her.

The girl came near her and whispered, "Are you happy? I killed your fake family for you" she said as she sat on the opposite chair of me.

"Well, it's time I introduce myself," the girl said as she leaned on the table and looked at me with a smirk.

"Hello, I am Willow. It's nice to finally meet you" the girl that resembled me told and brought her right hand for a handshake.

The moment Willow saw the identical girl's eyes, she knew she was a complete psychopath and it wasn't going to be a nice meeting.

End

9 798887 493572

Printed by Libri Plureos GmbH in Hamburg,
Germany